ITINERARY

1. Bristol
2. London
3. Compiègne
4. Paris
5. Cannes
6. Rome
7. Venice
8. Madrid
9. Barcelona
10. Vienna
11. Athens
12. Amsterdam
13. Home

Vienna, Austria

Venice, Italy

Rome, Italy

Athens, Greece

To Clancy, the cat that inspired the story

Special thanks to Chesley McLaren, who read the manuscript, joyfully responded, and spurred me on.
And my thanks to Ann Kelley, editor extraordinaire, who brought the book to life.

También gracias a mi familia y a los lectores jovenes del mundo quiénes continúan inspirándome.—C.L.

For Eliza and Tess—K.B.

Published in the United States by Schwartz & Wade Books, an imprint of Random House Children's Books, a division of Random House, Inc., New York. · Text copyright © 2008 by Caroline Lazo · Illustrations copyright © 2008 by Kyrsten Brooker · All rights reserved. · Schwartz & Wade Books and colophon are trademarks of Random House, Inc. · Visit us on the Web! www.randomhouse.com/kids · Educators and librarians, for a variety of teaching tools, visit us at www.randomhouse.com/teachers

Library of Congress Cataloging-in-Publication Data · Lazo, Caroline Evensen. · Someday when my cat can talk / Caroline Lazo ; illustrated by Kyrsten Brooker. — 1st ed. p. cm. · Summary: A girl imagines what her cat would tell her about its exotic travels to such places as the foggy English coast, Spanish bullfights, and an art gallery in Montmartre, France. Includes facts about the places mentioned. · ISBN 978-0-375-83754-8 (trade) — ISBN 978-0-375-93754-5 (lib. bdg.) · [1. Cats—Fiction. 2. Voyages and travels—Fiction. 3. Imagination—Fiction. 4. Stories in rhyme.] I. Brooker, Kyrsten, ill. II. Title. · PZ8.3L396 2008 · [E]—dc22 · 2006101809

The text of this book is set in Lomba.
The illustrations are rendered in collage and oil paint.
Book design by Rachael Cole

9378

PRINTED IN CHINA
10 9 8 7 6 5 4 3 2 1
First Edition

Random House Children's Books supports
the First Amendment and celebrates the right to read.

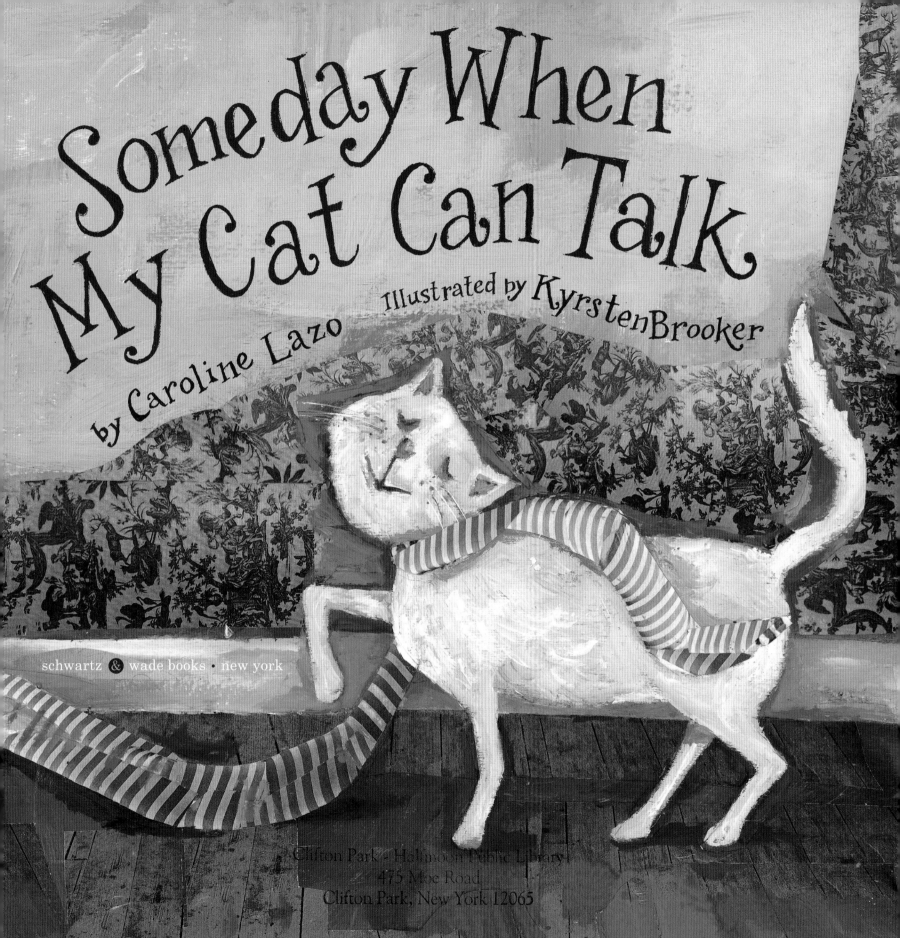

Someday When My Cat Can Talk

by Caroline Lazo   Illustrated by KyrstenBrooker

schwartz & wade books · new york

Someday when my cat can talk . . .

He'll tell me why he loves to hide
disguised among the flowers.
He'll talk about the basset hound
that spies on him for hours.

He'll tell me how much fun it is
to outrun the fastest mouse.
And he'll brag about the bat he caught
as it swooped above the house.

He'll purr about the seashore,
where his paws sink into sand.
And he'll gab about the fish he found
that washed up on the land.

He'll tell me how he hopped a ship
and where he stowed away.
He'll cheer the wind that blew his fur
as he sailed beyond the bay.

He'll recall the fog on England's coast,
where seagulls wander free.
And he'll tell me if it's really true
that British cats drink tea.

He'll muse about the mice that play
inside old palace walls
and how he liked to dine on them
in dimly lighted halls.

He'll sparkle when he speaks of France,
where he had such fun on wheels.
But he'll frown upon the fashion shows
with all the pointy heels.

He'll recall the wiry mousetrap
that he twisted into art,
and he'll boast about the prize he won
at a gallery in Montmartre.

He'll speak fondly of the snail he met
while camping out near Cannes.
And he'll whisper why she's hiding
from the chef at Café Sands.

He'll complain about the rabbits
that chased him into Rome.
But he'll rave about the stars that burst
above St. Peter's dome.

He'll tell me why the pigeons flock
to crumbs in St. Mark's Square.
And he'll crow about the gondolas
that took him everywhere.

He'll talk about events in Spain—
like bullfights every spring.
And he'll praise himself for stopping one
by jumping in the ring.

He'll relive the Spanish soccer games
when he played just like a pro
and all the señoritas yelled,

"¡Qué magnífico!"

He'll recall Vienna's Opera House
and the bird he met backstage.
And he'll tell me why she sings with joy
though locked inside her cage.

Fabulous Me!

He'll salute the awesome athletes
who awakened ancient Greece.
And he'll chat about the torch parade
he marched in for world peace.

He'll remember Holland's tulips
that the Dutch so proudly guard.
And he'll tell me if he missed me
and the flowers in our yard.

My cat will tell me all these things
when he talks to me someday.
Until then, when the sun goes down,
he always sneaks away.

He keeps his thoughts a secret
as he heads off toward the sea.
And no one knows just where he'll go—
except for you and me.

Facts Behind the Story

England

England is the largest of the four countries that make up the British Isles, and is the largest island in Europe. Because seagulls thrive on seacoasts, they flock here. Fog is common along the coasts. London, the country's capital, has about 113 foggy days each year.

Buckingham Palace in London is one of the Royal Family's many homes. Tea is a traditional British drink that is served at the palace and in homes throughout the country.

France

Every July, about 150 bicycle riders race in the famous Tour de France. But each day, people (and their pets!) can be seen touring the country on motorbikes, scooters, Rollerblades, and skateboards.

Each spring and fall, clothing designers from around the world show off their new styles—usually on models wearing high-heeled shoes—during Paris Fashion Week.

The arts flourish in France—in places like Montmartre, a section of Paris, the capital city, where owners of galleries (places to show off works of art) help artists sell their work and become known to the public, and also at the international film festival in Cannes, a popular resort city in southern France.

Snails (*escargots*) are delicacies that are served in many French restaurants.

Italy

Rabbits were first brought to Italy by Romans in the third century B.C. and have been a popular farm animal ever since. Rabbit meat is a basic part of the diet in this country.

St. Peter's Basilica is the largest church in the world and is known for its great dome, which brightens all of Rome, Italy's capital.

The city of Venice is built on about 118 islands in the Venetian Lagoon along the Adriatic Sea, and hundreds of bridges cross the canals there. People (and cats) often travel around the city in motorboats and gondolas, which are long, narrow, flat-bottomed boats.

St. Mark's Square, in the center of Venice, is a meeting place for residents and tourists—and pigeons, too!

Spain

Bullfighting is Spain's best-known and most unusual spectacle, but today many people think it is cruel to kill bulls—or any animals—for sport, and hope it will end soon. Soccer—or *fútbol* in Spanish—is the country's most popular sport, and many cities have stadiums that hold 100,000 or more fans.

Austria

Vienna, the capital of Austria, is famous for its music festivals honoring great composers who once lived and worked there, including Mozart, Beethoven, Schubert, Haydn, Mahler, and the Strauss family. The Vienna Opera House attracts music lovers from many nations and is one of the city's most treasured buildings.

Greece

The first Olympic Games (athletic contests) were held in 776 B.C. on the plains of Olympia in southern Greece. The festivals honored Zeus, king of the gods in Greek mythology, and took place every four years. In 1924 winter sports were added, and in 1994 the event switched to a two-year cycle, with winter and summer games alternating.

The Olympics take place in different cities around the world and include many sports, from boxing to yachting in the summer games (in which approximately ten thousand athletes compete) to ice-skating and bobsledding in the winter games (with about two thousand contestants). The Olympic Games help to promote world peace as well as good sportsmanship.

Holland

Holland, or the Netherlands, ships its famous tulip bulbs—nearly four thousand varieties of them!—to countries around the world. Dutch is the language spoken in the Netherlands and is the name given to the country's people.